"Charlotte's still doing ma[...]
said Robina.

"Do you really think so?" asked Daisy.

"Yes," said Robina, "and it would serve
her right if she *did* turn into a frog."

"Perhaps we could make a frogspell,"
suggested Daisy hopefully. "What do you
think?" She gave her sister a shove.

"What did you just say?" said Robina.

"I said, we could make a frogspell."

"No," said Robina. "No, what we want
is a dogspell."

YOUNG CORGI BOOKS

Young Corgi books are perfect when you are looking for great books to read on your own. They are full of exciting stories and entertaining pictures. There are funny books, scary books, spine-tingling stories and mysterious ones. Whatever your interests you'll find something in Young Corgi to suit you: from families to football, from animals to ghosts. The books are written by some of the most famous and popular of today's children's authors, and by some of the best new talents, too.

Whether you read one chapter a night, or devour the whole book in one sitting, you'll love Young Corgi books. The more you read, the more you'll want to read!

Other Young Corgi books to get your teeth into:
FUNNY FRANK by Dick King-Smith
PIGFACE by Catherine Robinson
SLEEPOVERS by Jacqueline Wilson

Dogspell

Helen Dunwoodie

Illustrated by Ruth Rivers

YOUNG CORGI

DOGSPELL
A YOUNG CORGI BOOK : 9780552558976

Published in Great Britain by Corgi Books,
an imprint of Random House Children's Books

This edition published 2003

Set in 16/20pt Bembo Schoolbook

Corgi Books are published by Random House Children's Books,
61–63 Uxbridge Road, London W5 5SA,
A Random House Group Company

Addresses for Random House Group Ltd companies outside the UK
can be found at: www.randomhouse.co.uk

THE RANDOM HOUSE GROUP Limited Reg. No. 954009
www.**kids**at**random**house.co.uk

A CIP catalogue record for this book is available from the British Library

Printed and bound in Great Britain by
Cox & Wyman Ltd, Reading, Berkshire.

With thanks to the
Scottish Arts Council

And for the original Robina
to whom I promised a book
H.D.

Chapter One

"I wish you girls would stop looking so bored," said Mum. "You know I have to go shopping before we go to the pool."

"We wouldn't be bored if we had a dog," whined Daisy.

"And you wouldn't have to take us swimming 'cause we'd be playing with our dog," said Robina. "You could be sitting down with a cup of coffee and the papers."

"Nice try," said Mum, "but if we had a dog, I know who'd end up looking after it. Now, stay here without moving one centimetre until I come back. And don't disturb your father. He says he's working."

And Mum stomped off, her big squashy sandals going kerthump on the sitting-room carpet. She was in a bad mood because Dad had brought work home. He usually took the girls swimming on Saturday mornings.

"What kind of dog would you like?" Robina asked Daisy. She sat down on the sofa and began to practise not moving, as Mum had ordered.

"A poodle," said Daisy. "A sweet little curly poodle." Daisy had curly hair. If only she had a poodle, she and her pet would match. People would look at them in the street. "What a lovely little girl! What a dear little dog!" they would say.

"Yeugh!" sneered Robina. "Poodles are so soppy!"

"So what would you wish for then?"

"A big, lolloping Afghan hound," said Robina. If only she had an Afghan hound, they would race together through the park. The wind would blow back the dog's long ears and her long ponytail.

"That's just silly," said Daisy. "An Afghan hound would need loads of exercise and mountains of food."

"Not as silly as a wussy poodle." Without moving from the sofa, Robina slid along and kicked her sister.

"Mum said not to move!"

"Who's moving? I'm still sitting here, aren't I?"

"If I had a poodle, it would bite you!" shouted Daisy.

"You're making a noise now," said Robina. "You'll disturb Dad."

Daisy, who was the younger, knew that Robina had somehow *made* her be noisy, but once she had started, it was hard to stop. "And it would bite your hairy old Afghan hound!"

"Would not."

The door opened. "What are you kids yelling about?" Charlotte, their big sister, was looking at them scornfully. She was wearing her best jeans and tightest top, with a flowery clip in her shiny, straight hair.

"Nothing," said Daisy and Robina together.

Charlotte sniffed. "So why aren't you swimming, tadpoles?"

"If we're tadpoles, you must be a frog by now," said Robina.

Charlotte sniffed again. "I'm going down town. And remember – I'LL KNOW IF YOU'VE BEEN IN MY ROOM!"

"How will you know?" asked Daisy. "Have you got a secret video camera?"

"Don't need it," said Charlotte. "I'll be able to *smell* if you've been in there. I'm teaching myself to be a witch, remember. I've got magic powers." And away she swept.

"Huh," said Daisy. "Some witch. Not one of her spells has worked."

"I know," said Robina. "She made a magic potion to cure her spots and they got worse."

"And she burned a hole in her carpet when she lit a special candle which was supposed to get her a boyfriend."

"But nothing happened."

"And Mum was furious about the carpet!"

Both girls fell back on the sofa, giggling.

"And Dad said that was the last bit of magic he wanted under his roof," said Robina. "I bet that's why she doesn't want us to go into her room. She's still doing magic in secret."

"Do you really think so?" asked Daisy.

"Yes," said Robina, "and it would serve her right if she *did* turn into a frog."

"Perhaps we could make a frogspell," suggested Daisy hopefully. "What do you think?" she gave her sister a shove.

"What did you just say?" said Robina.

"I said, we could make a frogspell."

"No," said Robina. "No, what we want is a dogspell."

Chapter Two

"There isn't a book called *Making Wishes Come True*."

The girls were in Charlotte's room, looking at her bookcase.

Daisy, who was still young enough to be proud of being able to read, read aloud: "*The Teenage Witch's Handbook, Spells for Young Lovers, Magic for Health and Happiness*."

"Let's try this one," Robina took down *Everyday Magic*. "All we want is a nice, easy wishing spell."

"But if the spells don't work for Charlotte, why should they work for us?"

"I didn't say it was going to *work*. I just think it's worth trying." Robina leafed through the book. "Look, this is just what we need! 'Bring Your Dream to Life.'"

"Let me see." Daisy looked over her shoulder. "We need a glass bowl full of spring water, a bunch of white flowers—"

"– a clear crystal and a stick of burning incense," finished Robina.

"But we're not allowed matches," said Daisy.

This was a problem.

"I know," said Robina. "I'm allowed

to boil the kettle and make tea. I'll make a mug of herb tea, and the steam will do instead of incense smoke."

"And we can borrow this crystal of Charlotte's."

"There's a glass bowl in the kitchen!"

"And we can pick flowers from the garden!"

Daisy's round face was pink with excitement, while Robina had gone pale. Casting a spell was going to be easier than they had imagined.

But could it possibly work?

★

Ten minutes later the girls were
sitting cross-legged on the sitting-room
carpet. Between them they had placed
the bowl of water, the crystal, some
pale roses in a small vase, and a mug
of peppermint tea. Robina had
chosen mint because it was the
strongest.

"So what do we do now?" whispered
Daisy. She whispered because what
had started as a joke now felt serious.
Even a bit scary.

Robina looked at the book. "We
both gaze into the water, trying really
hard to imagine the thing we're

wishing for. Then we say:

> 'Spirits of the air and earth,
> May our wishes come to birth.
> Spirits of the fire and sea,
> As we wish, so may it be.'"

"OK." Daisy gave a small nervous cough.
Both girls stared into the glass bowl.

Robina thought so
hard about her Afghan
hound that she could
see its flowing coat and
large, tender eyes.

Daisy thought so hard about her
poodle that she could
feel its curly coat under
her palm and hear
the thump of its
tufted tail.

"Now the spell,"
commanded
Robina.

19

They both recited it. Then they held their breaths. The air was thick with longing. Suddenly they heard a car hoot outside, followed by hurried steps on the path, and Mum's voice calling, "Quick, girls, I'm double-parked!"

"I bet that's broken the spell!" cried Daisy. "We ought to have wished for longer. It'll never work now." Her eyes filled with tears. "Will it, Robina?"

Robina didn't say anything. She got up, her lips pressed tight together.

"Will it?"

"Don't know. Anyway, it was only a silly old spell."

"Only a silly old spell," echoed Daisy. The car hooted again.

"Come on," said Robina. "Shut the door behind you. We'll clear up that stuff when we come home."

And grabbing their swimming things, they ran outside.

In the empty room, the water in the glass bowl quivered as the front door slammed. A few rose petals fell to the floor, and the peppermint steam drifted lazily around the magic circle.

Chapter Three

"You go in, girls, I'll need to drive round the block to find a parking space."

It was two hours later. Robina and Daisy, their damp hair smelling of chlorine, jumped out of the car and ran up the path.

Robina unlocked the front door. "Dad, we're home! Are you still working?"

"Can we disturb you yet?"

There was no reply.

"Dad's not here," said Daisy. "Look, his study door's open, but the room's empty."

Dad's study was really the cupboard under the stairs.

"Funny," said Robina. "Where can he be?"

Then the girls heard it.

From inside the sitting room.

A bark.

They both jumped, Daisy right out of her flip-flops, while Robina's ponytail almost swished against the ceiling.

"*What was that?*" Daisy's words came out in a throaty whisper.

"I – I don't know."

There was another deep, sonorous
Woof, followed by the sound of
something scrabbling at the door.

Something big.

Something with claws.

"It sounded like – like . . ."

"I know, like – a sort of . . ."

They looked at one another.

"A dog," breathed Daisy.

"It can't be," said Robina. Now she
knew what grown-ups meant when
they said they felt faint.

"Go on, open the door," said Daisy.

The thing was now whining as well
as scrabbling. How big was it? Did it
have teeth?

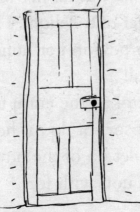

"It was your idea," continued Daisy, "and anyway, you're the eldest."

Very, very cautiously, Robina crept up to the door. Her lips were dry, but her hand, when she touched the doorknob, was sticky and damp. Then, scarcely breathing, she pushed the door open.

An absolutely enormous dog bounded out of the room. It ran round the sisters three times and then sat down, its immense plumed tail sweeping backwards and forwards across the floor. Finally, politely, it raised its front paw.

Robina let out all her breath in a sigh of relief and delight. Then she took the slender paw in her hand. "Oh, he's so beautiful!"

Daisy stroked the curly black head. "But what sort of dog is he?"

Robina let go of the paw. "What sort of dog did you wish for?"

"A poodle, of course. What about you?"

"An Afghan hound."

"So what we've got is—?"

"Yes. This dog's a mixture of our wishes. He's an – an Afoodle."

"The spell worked?"

"The spell worked."

Both girls suddenly felt that they had to sit down.

And their new friend, who was easily as big as an Afghan hound, but covered in a wild, curly poodle coat, sat down with them.

Chapter Four

After a few amazed moments of
stroking the Afoodle, Robina felt
stronger and got to her feet. "We must
show him to Dad."

"Why didn't he hear the barking?
Where is he?"

But Dad wasn't upstairs, nor in the
garden.

"Here's a clue in his study," said
Robina. "His address book is lying on
his desk, open at the letter Z."

"Z?"

"Yes, and there's only one entry. Gabriel Ziggy."

Woof! The Afoodle barked once and waved his tail.

"Was Dad phoning Gabriel?" said Robina.

Woof, answered the Afoodle.

"Who's Gabriel Ziggy?" asked Daisy.

"He's that friend of Mum and Dad's who's getting married. Remember, Dad said his girlfriend looks exactly like her Pekinese – same little squashy face."

The Afoodle barked again, ran into the sitting room and sat down in the centre of the magic circle.

"Oh, Robina, he's trying to tell us something!"

"Dad was on the phone and then he came in here?"

The Afoodle gave a small, eager whine.

"Dad came in here, and—?"

The Afoodle barked again. Then he bent his noble head and lapped some water from the enchanted bowl.

"Dad came in here and drank some water out of a bowl on the floor?" said Daisy. "I don't think so."

The Afoodle gave another whine and pawed at the carpet.

"We're trying to understand, honestly," said Robina. "Oh, if only you could talk! Dad came in here, he wandered into the middle of the spell—"

She stopped as an unbelievably awful thought came to her. She looked at Daisy and Daisy looked back, the same idea making her shiver.

"Oh, Robina, you don't think—?"

"No, it's impossible."

"When we went out, we didn't leave some magic behind us, all sticky like a cobweb . . . ?"

"Of course not. And anyway, that dog looks nothing like Dad."

The Afoodle slurped water on the carpet and, turning round, knocked over both the mug of tea and the roses.

"It is Dad!" wailed Daisy. "That's exactly what he would do."

The Afoodle looked up into their
sorrowful faces.

"But we don't know for sure," said
Robina.

Then they heard the front door open.

"Hello, girls," called Mum. "Where's
your father?"

Chapter Five

"We – we don't know," said Daisy.

"He's not in here," said Robina,
hurrying into the hall.

She tried to shut the door behind her,
but she wasn't quick enough.

"What's that noise?" said Mum.

The Afoodle had given a small,
excited bark.

Mum pushed the door open. She saw
the spilt water, the trampled flowers, her
red-faced daughters – and a huge
hairy, untidy dog. "Just what is going
on? And where did that . . . animal
come from?"

"He's not an animal!" cried Daisy.

"At least, we don't think so," said Robina.

"Then what exactly is it?" Mum had gone as pink as the girls, and her eyes were bright and hot.

"He's . . ."

"He's . . ."

"He's not an *ordinary* dog exactly," said Robina.

"That's obvious," said Mum. "I've never seen such a big, bristly brute in all my life. He's like an animated hearth rug."

The Afoodle whined.

"Oh, Mum, you've hurt his feelings!"

"We love him, who— whatever he is." Daisy flung her arms round the Afoodle's neck.

"But what's he doing here? And where's your father?"

The Afoodle whined again. Then he looked up at Mum and lovingly, hopefully, raised his front paw.

Mum looked back. "At least he's been well trained," she said. She looked harder still. "It's odd, but he seems familiar. It's almost as though I'd seen him before somewhere." Puzzled, she shook the Afoodle's paw.

The Afoodle gazed back with devotion, while Robina and Daisy watched helplessly.

"I simply can't place him," said Mum.

"Perhaps he reminds you of someone you've seen recently?" said Robina.

"Very, very recently," said Daisy.

"Someone who isn't here just now but ought to be?"

"What *are* you talking about?" said Mum. "The only person who isn't where he ought to be is your father."

Chapter Six

"But I am now. Well, girls, how do you like your new pet?"

For the second time in ten minutes, Daisy left her flip-flops embedded in the carpet while she sailed towards the ceiling. Robina was only just behind her.

Dad stood in the doorway, laughing heartily and a little nervously, with a plastic bag in either hand.

The Afoodle rushed to meet him, swishing his lovely tail, but it took a few minutes for the girls to recover their wits. Then they threw themselves on Dad, relieved at how safe and solid he felt in his old, weekend clothes.

"Dad, where have you been?"

"Where did the gorgeous dog come from?"

"Can we keep him?"

Dad put down the bags, which contained tins of dog food, and hugged daughters and Afoodle. He looked at Mum over their heads.

"Darling," she said, "we've discussed this. And we both agreed. No dog."

"But this isn't an ordinary dog," said Dad, his eyes as pleading as those of the Afoodle. "This is Gabriel's dog, Champion Prince Bertie of Breadalbane."

"Of course," said Mum. "That's where I've seen him before. At Gabriel's."

"Well, it turns out Bertie here is terrified of Gabriel's girlfriend's Pekinese, Shanghai Lily."

At the name Shanghai Lily, Prince Bertie shuddered.

"And I don't blame him," said Dad. "It's a horrid little thing, like a feather duster on wheels. But the girlfriend wouldn't be parted from her, so either they went, or Bertie did. Of course, Gabriel was heartbroken, but what else could he do?"

Prince Bertie howled, but very quietly. It was the saddest sound the girls had ever heard.

"How could he?" Robina's eyes were wet.

"Oh, Bertie, we'll make it up to you! You're a hundred times better than any old Peke," said Daisy.

Even Mum looked a little unhappy. "I can see it was a difficult decision to have to make," she said, "but why did he give him to you – or no, I bet you offered to take him?"

It was Dad's turn to blush. "Well, I was just phoning Gabriel to see if he fancied a game of tennis—"

"Tennis?" interrupted Mum. "Excuse me, but I thought you said you were going to be working hard the entire morning?"

"But I did, I was," protested Dad. This was going to be tennis – er – next week. Anyway, we were chatting and he told me about his problem, so I said, what a terrible dilemma, and what about Battersea Dogs' Home – " Bertie shuddered again, his long coat rippling – "and Gabriel said, no, no, he couldn't put his oldest, dearest friend into a home, and so one thing led to another . . ."

Everybody looked at Mum. Daisy clasped her hands dramatically, Robina allowed a tear to trickle down her cheek, and Dad shuffled a bit.

Prince Bertie, once again showing his great intelligence, lay down at Mum's

feet and put his paws over his nose.
Every inch of his long, curly body
declared: Just see how good and quiet
I can be.

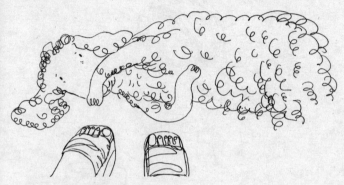

Mum gave in. "Oh, all right," she
snapped. "But don't expect *me* to take
him for walks or feed him or brush that
horrid thick coat."

The girls shrieked with joy. Prince
Bertie, too wise to bark, wagged his
tail. Dad kissed Mum and promised to
take Bertie and the girls for a long
walk every Sunday morning so that she
could have a lie-in.

"OK," said Mum, "and seeing as how
you've got to be good for the rest of

your lives, you can start by picking up all this rubbish. And what is my good fruit bowl doing on the carpet?"

"Just what I was wondering," said Dad. "I came in here when I'd finished work and saw all this stuff. I was going to clear it up but then it occurred to me to ring Gabriel."

Daisy and Robina felt their skin tingle.

"It was – er – we were . . ." Robina cleared her throat and tried again. "It

44

was a sort of spell. Out of one of Charlotte's books."

"Honestly," said Mum. "This magic nonsense of Charlotte's has gone far enough. She'll do something really silly one of these days."

"I'd call nearly burning the house down silly enough," said Dad.

"We'll just have to encourage her to grow out of it." said Mum. "And I certainly don't want you two growing into it."

"What was the spell for?" asked Dad.

Daisy burrowed her toes into the carpet. "A dog," she whispered. "A poodle."

"A dog," repeated Robina. "An Afghan hound."

The grown-ups burst out laughing.

"As though you could magic a dog out of thin air!" said Mum.

"Prince Bertie here's as solid as I am," said Dad, rubbing the dog's curly coat.

But you were standing in the magic circle when you decided to phone

Gabriel! Robina thought, but did not say this.

Mum and Dad were still laughing when the front door slammed.

"I'm home!" shouted Charlotte.

Chapter Seven

Charlotte always announced her return loudly so that the other, less important family members could start paying attention to her.

"Charlotte, come in here!"

"Charlotte, look what we've got!"

Robina and Daisy rushed towards the door as their big sister entered.

"What on earth is that?" Charlotte demanded, looking past them at Prince Bertie, while everyone looked at Charlotte. Looked very, very hard for a long, silent moment.

Then Prince Bertie gave a joyful bark of recognition and rushed at Charlotte in a swirl of long hair and hot doggy breath.

The reason for his enthusiasm was obvious. Since leaving in the morning, Charlotte had had her hair done. No longer shiny or straight, it now stood out on either side of her head in huge festoons of curls so that, in fact, she looked exactly like Prince Bertie himself.

"What have you done to your hair?" gasped Mum.

"It's good, isn't it?" said Charlotte. "There was a special offer on at Twist 'n' Curl. This is the latest style."

"But when did you—?" gulped Robina.

"What's this huge hound doing here?" said Charlotte, ignoring her sister. "I thought Mum said no dogs?"

"Yes, I did," said Mum. "Charlotte, that's not a perm, is it?"

"But when did you decide to get it done?" repeated Robina. Her big sister looked so extraordinary that it was hard not to laugh.

"Oh, about a couple of hours ago. I was passing Twist 'n' Curl and they had this poster in the window."

Robina and Daisy exchanged glances. Two hours ago, the very time when they'd been casting the spell!

"She looks exactly like a dog. Some sort of spaniel," whispered Daisy, giggling.

"A Chariel," Robina whispered back.

"It's not funny," said Mum. "Charlotte, you didn't answer my question."

Charlotte was now romping round the room with Bertie, her new curls bouncing out over her ears. "Don't worry, Mum," she said. "It's only semi-permanent."

Mum sighed.

"Shall I put the kettle on?" said Robina helpfully.

"We could make you a nice cup of

coffee," said Daisy.

"And we'll clear up all this stuff," said
Robina, picking up the crystal bowl.
"Come on, Daisy."

What she really meant was, we'd
better clear it up before something else
happens, because while Charlotte
hadn't actually changed into a dog, she
did look amazingly like one.

Dad was telling the story of Gabriel's
girlfriend all over again.

53

"So the tadpoles got their dearest wish," said Charlotte, when he'd finished, "and all due to the mean girlfriend."

"You could look at it like that," said Mum. "Just how semi is semi-permanent?"

"So what kind of dog is he?" said Charlotte, carefully not answering Mum's question. "I've never seen anything like him."

"Of course you haven't," said Dad. "He's a very rare breed."

Daisy and Robina looked up from their tidying.

"He's not a . . . ?"

"He can't really be a . . . ?"

"He's a Briand," said Dad.
"That's a special sort of French
mountain dog. Big and strong, and with
a thick coat to keep out the cold."

"So that's what he is," said Robina,
mopping up the spilt water with a cloth
she'd brought from the kitchen. "We
knew he wasn't any old ordinary dog,
didn't we, Daisy?"

Daisy nodded.

"And if I were still wishing for a dog," continued Robina, "he's exactly the sort I'd wish for."

"Me too," said Daisy. "This absolute sort and nothing else." And she hugged Prince Bertie as hard as she could without hurting him.

"What are all these flowers doing on the floor?" asked Charlotte, noticing for the first time the remains of the spell.

"These silly girls were trying to get a dog by magic," said Dad. "They cast some spell or other."

"Wow!" said Charlotte. "And it actually worked!" For the first time ever she looked at her sisters with respect.

"What nonsense!" snapped Mum.
"Of course it didn't work. It was sheer
coincidence that your father was talked
into getting a dog on the same day as
the girls pretended to do some magic.
And it was your fault, Charlotte, that
they even tried."

Charlotte wasn't listening. "What
spell did you use?" she asked Robina.

"It was called 'Bring Your Dream to Life,'" said Robina. "I'm afraid we had to go into your room to get the book. We're frightfully sorry—"

"That doesn't matter," said Charlotte. "I've never tried that one. What do you need – white flowers, bowl of water—?"

"No more magic," said Mum. "Please. Now, we'd better fix up a bed for this fellow." She tried to look severely at Bertie, but when he gazed back with his melting toffee eyes, she had to smile. "Oh look at him! Who could resist?" she said.

Dad smiled too. "I'll go and fetch his basket from Gabriel's now you've brought the car back." He gave Mum a loving squeeze. "I knew you'd come round to Bertie once you'd seen him."

"Oh, Bertie, we all love you now!" cried Daisy, hugging him all over again.

"We certainly do," said Charlotte thoughtfully. "Was that a spell from *Everyday Magic*?"

"Mm. Yes," admitted Robina. She wondered what would happen if Charlotte cast a spell which actually worked. Would her skin become lily-smooth? Would a wonderful boyfriend appear on the doorstep, a boyfriend with the latest jeans and trainers and – and curly hair to match her new look? Robina began to giggle again.

"What's so funny?" said Daisy.

Robina joined her on the floor beside Bertie. "Tell you later," she whispered. Then she said aloud, "Darling Prince Bertie, you're the dog of our dreams!"

"We'll never be bored again, ever, ever, ever."

"We'll never moan and complain."

"You'd better not," said Mum, but she was smiling.

"All our wishes have come true!" cried Daisy.

And Champion Prince Bertie of Breadalbane twirled around three times, lay down amongst the magic rose petals, and fell asleep.

THE END

ANNIE AND THE ALIENS
Emily Smith

Watch out!
There's an alien in the garden!

Annie is furious. Her brothers have banned her from their room and insist on keeping secrets from her. But Annie won't be left out. When she finds out what the boys are whispering about, they'll get an astronomical surprise!

An entertaining story from the author of *The Shrimp* (Smarties Gold Medal-winner) and *Astrid, the Au Pair from Outer Space* (Smarties Silver Medal-winner)

ISBN 0 552 54853 7